PUFFIN BOOKS

THE GARDEN OF EMPRESS CASSIA

Mimi laid the box on the bench and opened it carefully. Inside were rows and rows of coloured pastels that shimmered in the light. She rolled them under her fingertips and her imagination began to fill with amazing pictures.

When Mimi is given a box of magical pastels, she discovers that she can draw the Garden of Empress Cassia – a drawing so beautiful and real that people are transported inside it. But the pastels are ancient, mysterious and powerful, and in the wrong hands, can be very dangerous . . .

*I would like to thank Hazel Edwards for all her support
and encouragement while writing this book.*

THE GARDEN OF EMPRESS CASSIA

GABRIELLE WANG

with illustrations by the author

PUFFIN BOOKS

PUFFIN BOOKS

Published by the Penguin Group
Penguin Books Ltd, 80 Strand, London WC2R 0RL, England
Penguin Putnam Inc., 375 Hudson Street, New York, New York 10014, USA
Penguin Books Australia Ltd, 250 Camberwell Road, Camberwell, Victoria 3124, Australia
Penguin Books Canada Ltd, 10 Alcorn Avenue, Toronto, Ontario, Canada M4V 3B2
Penguin Books India (P) Ltd, 11 Community Centre, Panchsheel Park,
New Delhi – 110 017, India
Penguin Books (NZ) Ltd, Cnr Rosedale and Airborne Roads, Albany, Auckland,
New Zealand
Penguin Books (South Africa) (Pty) Ltd, 24 Sturdee Avenue, Rosebank 2196, South Africa

Penguin Books Ltd, Registered Offices: 80 Strand, London WC2R 0RL, England

www.penguin.com

Published in Australia by Penguin Books Australia, 2002
Published in Great Britain by Puffin Books, 2003

1

Text and illustrations copyright © Gabrielle Wang, 2002
Designed by Marina Messiha, Penguin Design Studio
All rights reserved

The moral right of the author/illustrator has been asserted

Set in 12/18 Bembo

Made and printed in England by Clays Ltd, St Ives plc

British Library Cataloguing in Publication Data
A CIP catalogue record for this book is available from the British Library

ISBN 0–141–31649–7

For my children, Lei Lei and Ren

Contents

The Shop of Strange Smells

There were those at school who smelt of tomato sauce, others of garlic. And of course there was no avoiding the stench of BO after the cross-country run. But Mimi had a curious smell that no one could recognize.

Mimi Lu lived in a two-storey shop that seemed to float on a cloud of strange smells. She was embarrassed enough that her home stank like a compost heap on a hot day, but the odour seeped into everything – her clothes, her pigtails, her skin – and could even be detected on her breath. Her parents forced her to drink all kinds of disgusting brews. The only way to get them down was to hold her nose until the very last swallow.

At school she was called Smelly-Loo. Kids complained if they were asked to share a desk with her. She never told her mum or dad about the bullying. They wouldn't understand. They might as well have come from Mars.

'Remember, Mimi, you are Chinese. Be proud of it.' The words rattled around inside her brain. They were empty words that didn't belong to her.

How can I be proud? They speak English with a funny accent that makes them sound really dumb. And other kids live in a proper house with grass and a garden. All I have is the footpath out on the street.

Mimi sat at the old laminex table in the kitchen staring at her navy-blue school hat. She was remembering what Miss O'Dell, her art teacher, had told her that day about *chiaroscuro* – how to paint light and dark. The more she looked at her hat, the more it looked like a mountain range with hills and valleys.

Through the red curtains that separated the shop from the living quarters, Mimi could see her father putting on his clinic coat, ready for the first patient.

Ding ding-a-ling. The shop door opened.

'Dr Lu, I'm in a bit of a hurry. Can you see me now?' came a voice used to giving orders.

Uh oh. Mimi hid behind her maths book.

'Of course, Miss Sternhop,' replied Mimi's dad.

Miss Sternhop rapped her walking stick on the concrete floor. She was a solid lady with short, straight brown hair and two massive trunks for legs. The only thin part of her body was her lips. If Miss Sternhop ever collided with a car, it would be the car that suffered the most damage.

She placed her wrist on a small cushion. Dr Lu felt her pulse. Was it weak or strong, stringy or full? He wrote on a pad in Chinese characters.

'See your tongue, please,' said Dr Lu.

Miss Sternhop opened her mouth wide and poked out her tongue. It was purple and thick and swollen at the edges.

She looks like an iguana from the Galapagos Islands. Mimi stifled a giggle.

On the back wall of the shop stood an antique wooden cabinet, with one hundred box-like drawers. The cabinet once belonged to Mimi's grandfather in China. He was a herbalist too. Dr Lu didn't know how old it was, but he was always finding secrets from other people's lives. Once he found a carved jade bracelet hidden in a secret panel at the back of a drawer. It was so tiny only a child could have worn it. There was a letter too, folded into the shape of a bird and pushed through the centre of the bracelet.

'Aiya, family so poor, have to give away precious baby daughter. Before in China many people like this.' Mrs Lu touched her heart.

Mimi wondered what it would be like to live in China. *If I was born there, I'd look like everyone else. I'd fit right in.*

Dr Lu pulled one drawer halfway out and grabbed a handful of dried mistletoe. From other drawers he pulled out slices of fragrant angelica, liquorice root and creamy-white grains of Job's tears. He weighed each herb separately, then divided them evenly into four paper packages.

'This good for arthritis,' said Dr Lu. 'Drink two times every day.'

'How's Mimi doing at school?' asked Miss Sternhop.

Mimi slid down in her chair.

'Not good,' Dr Lu replied, shaking his head. 'She draw too much.'

'That was her trouble when she was in my class last year.' Miss Sternhop hardly moved her tight, thin lips. 'Never concentrated. In my experience, you've got to come down hard on children like that.' She banged the counter with a clenched fist, as if she were squashing a helpless bug.

'See you in a month, Dr Lu.' Miss Sternhop strode out to join the stream of life on the street.

When Miss Sternhop was well out of earshot, Mimi yelled from the kitchen, 'I hate old Stir-em-up. She never liked me.'

'Hate not good word, Mimi.'

'But I do. She's mean. The whole school was glad to see her go.'

'Why you late today?' Dr Lu flicked the counter with a feather duster then walked through the red curtains.

'I told you already, Dad. Miss O'Dell is giving me special art classes after school. She says I have real talent.' Mimi hadn't made a big deal of it. She knew her dad would be angry.

'You need to concentrate on school work . . . not painting,' he said, suddenly breaking into Chinese. He did this whenever he was serious or angry. 'Painting is not a respected profession.'

'But I love drawing and painting, Dad,' she replied in English. Two years ago, Mimi had decided never to speak Chinese again. 'I'm Australian, *not* Chinese,' she had said defiantly. She knew it made her parents angry, but it was the one thing in her life she had control over.

Her dad waved his hand towards the yellowing

photograph hanging above the altar table in the hallway and frowned at her. 'Your *nai nai* and *gong gong* are watching, waiting for you to honour the family name. You have no brother, so it is up to you to please the ancestors.'

'Oh, phooey,' Mimi said softly, then looked up, hoping the ancestors were hard of hearing. She felt the disapproving stare of her grandmother and grandfather on their ancestral cloud. *Isn't burning incense every day enough for you? Don't you know that other kids' parents say, 'well done, you did your best'. They're always being told how great they are. I get ninety-eight for a maths test and Dad says it's not good enough. All he ever does is criticize . . .*

'Tell your teacher you are busy after school. No more wasting time.' Mimi's dad broke into her thoughts.

'But, Dad, that's not fair,' she replied angrily.

Dr Lu sat down at his desk, his back blocking the conversation. It was no use. He had shut her out as usual. Mimi had learnt long ago that Chinese children never argue with their parents.

She stared at her maths book as tears melted the black digits into blurry grey blobs. *Why did I have to be born into a Chinese family?*

The Gift

Traffic was busy this morning on Rumba Street. Trams were banked up along the track like large green caterpillars playing follow-the-leader. Two men stood on the roof of a yellow tramway's truck, fixing the power lines overhead, black wires playing noughts and crosses against the sky.

'Hey, ching chong,' a voice yelled from a passing car.

'*Unfortunate beings!*' Mimi muttered, to keep out the hurt.

'People like that very unfortunate,' her mum would say. 'Their parents no teach them right or wrong.'

As Mimi arrived at the school gate, the bell started ringing. This week's number one hit, 'ME-YOW' by

The Furballs, was blaring from loudspeakers into the assembly area.

'I thought we could do some pottery today, Mimi,' said Miss O'Dell, walking beside her down the asphalt path. 'I fired up the kiln yesterday.'

Miss O'Dell's rosy cheeks stood out like little pink balloons as she smiled at Mimi. Her skin was smooth and soft, and when she spoke it was as though she were singing a gentle Irish lullaby.

'Dad won't let me come any more,' Mimi replied sadly.

'Why ever not?'

'He says I draw too much. I have to concentrate on school work.'

'My, that's a shame. But maybe if you work really hard, he might change his mind and let you come back. Give it a go, all right? Why don't you drop by the art room on your way home anyway. I've got something to give you.'

After morning assembly, Mimi slipped into her wooden desk beside Josh Rudd. She liked Josh. Everyone did. He had a broad smiling face and spiky fair hair and his voice would crack in mid-sentence. But best of all, he never called her Smelly-Loo. Instead he called her M.

Josh was extremely untidy. His books would start in a nice neat pile at nine fifteen. By nine sixteen, they would slowly spread, like molten lava, across both desks, on to the seat, then finally spill over on to the floor. By three thirty, Mimi's feet would be surrounded by books, pencils, pens, rubbers and rulers, all belonging to Josh. But Mimi didn't mind a bit.

At lunchtime, Mimi sat by herself in her usual spot under the peppercorn tree, swinging her legs to keep away the flies.

'Hey there, Smelly-Loo . . . what ya got for lunch today?' chanted Gemma Johnson, the leader of the 'cool' group. She winked at her two sidekicks, Phoebe and Eliza. Gemma always wore her hair high in a ponytail which she would deliberately swing from side to side to attract attention. Especially the attention of Josh Rudd. She was jealous that Mimi got to sit next to him in class. 'What a waste,' she told everyone.

Mimi grimaced, desperately trying to hide her Thermos before Gemma could make fun of it. But it was too late.

'She's eating flied lice!' Phoebe pointed and laughed.

'Oh, puke,' said Gemma, sticking her fingers down

her throat. 'And look at these primitive eating sticks.' She snatched Mimi's chopsticks and rolled them under her shoe. 'There, all nicely sterilized. Why don't you use a knife and fork like civilized people?'

Eliza and Phoebe giggled. 'Seeya, Smells,' they chorused and ran off towards the oval.

Why won't Mum give me a plain old sandwich like everyone else?

Mimi had pleaded with her mum to pack *normal* lunches, but her mum didn't understand what the problem was. 'Hot fried rice is surely better than a cold sandwich for lunch,' she had told Mimi. 'Cold food is not good for the stomach.'

Suddenly, Mimi had lost her appetite.

As soon as the bell rang for dismissal, Mimi grabbed her bag and raced to the art room. She loved the thick and slightly sickly smell of paint, and the brushes standing up in their containers like bunches of hairy flowers. The shelves were stacked with a new delivery of coloured paper, but it was the pure white paper that Mimi loved the best, lying there waiting to be given new life.

Miss O'Dell stood on a bench, pinning up giant papier mâché faces with bulbous eyes and hairy noses.

'Hello, Mimi,' she said, her mouth studded with drawing pins. 'Come in, I'll just be a sec.' She spat the pins into her hand and climbed down, then cocked her head to one side as she looked into Mimi's face.

'Something's bothering you, I can tell.'

'It doesn't matter.'

'Come on, what is it?'

Mimi wasn't used to telling *outside* people her feelings. 'We Chinese keep them to ourselves,' her mum always said, 'that way we never lose face.' But Mimi did feel a closeness with Miss O'Dell that she never felt with her parents.

'I hate being a banana.' The words echoed around the art room.

'A banana?'

'You know . . . yellow on the outside and white on the inside. I wish I didn't look Chinese because I don't feel Chinese. I feel just like everyone else. I hate it.'

Miss O'Dell smiled her soft smile. 'I know it's hard being different, but that's what's wonderful about you. You are a Chinese Australian just like I'm an Irish Australian. And I think we're lucky.'

'I don't think so. Someone like Gemma Johnson is lucky. She fits right in.'

'You might feel that way now, but as you grow older you will see how you can choose the best from both cultures. Sit down, Mimi.' Miss O'Dell pulled out a stool. 'You know, there's something else, apart from your Chineseness, that makes you different from others. You are an artist. You see the world in a special way – and you paint with your heart. Few people can do that.' Miss O'Dell's eyes brightened. 'I've got an idea. If you don't mind giving up your lunchtime, how about coming in twice a week, say Mondays and Thursdays? Your father surely wouldn't object to that.'

'Oh, Miss O'Dell, that'd be so great.' *Dad'll never find out and I'll be able to eat my lunch in peace*, thought Mimi.

'I've been meaning to give you something for a long while now. I think the time is just right.'

Miss O'Dell went over to her bag and pulled out an oblong object wrapped in a purple silk scarf. She handed it to Mimi.

'Open it,' she whispered, as if she were about to share a secret.

Mimi let the silk slip away. It was a long wooden box with a beautiful carving of a miniature oriental garden on the lid, with willows and pavilions and bridges crossing lakes. As Mimi ran her fingers over the honey-gold surface, it was like touching the finest silk or the smooth skin of a newborn baby. Flowing Chinese characters were carved around the sides and inlaid with mother of pearl. Mimi read each character out loud:

> *Empress Cassia*
> *Supreme Ruler of all China*
> *80 Sticks of the Finest China Pastels*
> *A Treasure for Some*
> *A Curse for Others*

That's funny, why would pastels be a curse? Mimi wondered, then put the thought out of her mind.

She laid the box on the bench and opened it carefully. Inside were rows and rows of coloured pastels that shimmered in the light. The colours were so delicate they looked as though they had been made from the gossamer wings of fairies.

Mimi rolled the pastels under her fingertips and her imagination began to fill with amazing pictures.

'You must promise me one thing, Mimi.' Miss O'Dell spoke in an unusually serious voice and a frown touched her brow.

'What is it, Miss O'Dell?'

'*No one* is to use the pastels but you. Look me in the eye, Mimi, and promise me now.'

'I promise, Miss O'Dell. I definitely won't let anyone use them. They're too precious. Thank you so much.' Impulsively, she gave Miss O'Dell a big hug. 'I'd better go or Dad'll be mad. Thanks for everything.'

Mimi carefully wrapped the box up in the silk scarf and raced out the door, her mind brimming with pictures. She couldn't wait to get home and start drawing.

Four Seasons in a Day

Mimi dumped her bag in the hallway and entered the kitchen. 'Hi, Mum, has Dad gone out?' she asked hopefully.

'Your daddy go Sydney. Uncle Ting in hospital.' Mrs Lu looked worried. She shook her head slowly. 'He not live long, Mimi.'

'Uncle Ting? But he's younger than Dad, isn't he?'

'His stomach no good — eat too much meat, too much greasy food.'

Mimi hadn't seen her uncle since she was six years old. She remembered how he had joked with her and recited beautiful Tang dynasty poems, each word rolling off his tongue like a polished pearl. How she wished her dad could be like him.

'Why didn't he ever come back to visit?' asked Mimi.

'Aiya . . .' sighed Mrs Lu. 'Your daddy angry. He say Uncle Ting lazy, because he not find good job. Lu family lose face, make ancestors unhappy.' She sighed again. 'Maybe they now make peace.'

'Will he die soon?'

'Doctor say any time. You want something eat, Mimi?'

'Later, Mum. I'm going outside to do a drawing for Uncle Ting, OK?'

Mimi took the box of Empress Cassia Pastels from her school bag and went out into the street. The footpath was her giant drawing board. Drawing would calm her heart when she was angry, or cheer her up when she was sad. And when she was happy, she would draw as freely as an eagle catching thermals in a clear blue sky.

Mimi knew all the regular shoppers by their shoes – and sometimes even by the sound of their footsteps. Mrs Jacobs always wore high heels. They made a *dock*, *dock*, *dock* sound as she hurried by. Those bright red shoes of hers with the pointy toes could be used as lethal weapons! And then there was Mr Honeybun. One day, when Mimi had been inspecting a tiny ant dragging an *enormous* breadcrumb across a crack in the footpath, she heard loud farts coming down the street. *How gross,* she thought, holding her breath as a man came limping towards her. *Twelve farts in a row. Should be in the* Guinness Book of Records.

It wasn't until a few weeks later that Mimi learnt Mr Honeybun's left leg had been blown off by a bomb in World War II. He had to wear a plastic leg held to his stump by suction. The limb didn't fit properly, so it made a farting noise as he walked. Now Mimi always said a special hello to Mr Honeybun.

Mimi knelt on the pavement and carefully opened the box of pastels. Once again, her imagination exploded with colour. Wonderful images of gardens floated into her mind. She took a shimmering sapphire blue and began to draw a pond. A soft summer breeze blew down the street, so Mimi drew gentle waves rippling around the shore. Long-necked swans dived for snails. Their tails bobbed on the water like fluffy white meringues.

Mimi already had a keen eye for detail, but today she even surprised herself. The two-dimensional world she had drawn in pastels on the footpath was truly beautiful.

'Dinner's ready, Mimi,' Mrs Lu called.

She was just packing up when Gemma and Phoebe passed by holding their noses and wrinkling up their faces.

'What's that disgusting smell?' Gemma said. 'Oh, hi, Mimi, I didn't see you there. Is your dad still giving people garden sweepings to boil up and drink?'

Phoebe giggled.

Why can't I stand up to her? Say something back, you wimp. But Mimi's words caught in her throat.

'Wanna come ghost hunting tonight?' Gemma asked, a smirk on her face. 'They say Ghost Gum Park is totally swarming with them.'

'No thank you,' said Mimi coldly.

'Your loss, our gain. Come on, Phoebs.' Gemma turned to leave, then spied the box of pastels lying on the footpath. 'Hey, these are cool. Where did you get them?' She bent down to take a closer look.

'Get away!' Mimi was surprised at the anger in her own voice. She rushed over and grabbed the box, holding it protectively to her chest, then ran into the shop leaving an indignant Gemma standing on the footpath, her mouth gaping.

The next day, Mimi was eager to beat the Saturday morning rush of shoppers. Last year, Wattle Valley Council had laid large concrete pavers along Rumba Street. It was a much better surface for Mimi to draw on than the old footpath. She was no longer restricted by the cracks, or the big black blobs of chewing gum that freckled the ground.

An idea had come to Mimi during the night. She wanted to draw the images before they dissolved into air. She opened the box of pastels. In her mind she saw spring flowers bursting into full bloom. She chose a pastel the colour of velvet moss on a rainforest floor in the early morning – and drew a crisp, cool spring day. A young woman jogged past, then stopped. She looked down at the drawing and wiped her brow with her sleeve. It was as if she could feel the coolness in the air. 'Great painting, kid,' she said, and dropped a dollar coin into the lid of the box. Before Mimi had a chance to return the money, the jogger was up the hill and out of sight. Another passer-by stopped to look into the painting. It was Mr Holes. Mimi didn't know his real name. She called him that because his coat was so full of holes it looked as though mice had mistaken it for cheese.

Mr Holes spent the night wherever he could find shelter from the wind and rain. Sometimes it was in a shop doorway, sometimes it was in a dumpster. He had no set place. He was a wanderer. Mr Holes scratched his head. His dreadlocks wriggled like thick, curly worms. What was he trying to remember?

By noon, more people gathered. Mimi drew a beach streaked with seaweed and dotted with laughing children. Above them, seagulls caught crusts in mid-air.

'Daddy,' said a small boy. 'I want to play too.' He struggled with his safety harness, trying to get out of his pusher. His father smiled. 'Beautiful day for a swim,' he said absent-mindedly, even though a curtain of cloud now covered the sky.

'I think I'll take the children down to the beach after lunch,' the lady standing next to him replied.

By late afternoon, Mimi was drawing the swirling leaves of autumn floating across golden hills. The crowd was two deep by now, but nobody pushed or shoved as they watched the Garden of Four Seasons grow. They were amazed at the colours and fine sensitive lines. There was something in the drawings that each person under-stood – as if a distant memory had been awakened. The perfume of roses floated in the air, even though there wasn't a rose within at least three miles. And if there was a lull in the traffic, was that the sound of a waterfall that could be heard cascading over rocks?

As dusk approached, Mimi completed the full cycle. A snowman, with a carrot nose and corks for eyes, bravely withstood the icy winds of winter. In the centre of the four drawings, she drew a *yin yang* symbol. Uncle Ting had shown Mimi this ancient image that went round and round into itself. It fascinated her as a little girl. He said that it represented the never-ending cycle of change in the universe – day turning into night, summer into winter, good into bad. And then the whole cycle was repeated all over again.

Mimi thought of Uncle Ting lying in hospital in the winter of his life. Would he be reborn to continue the cycle? Her mum believed that everyone came back to Earth many times. She was Buddhist. That's why she was a vegetarian and wouldn't even kill an ant. Mimi hoped it was true.

'Uncle Ting . . . the Garden of Four Seasons is for you,' she whispered.

As the sun sank low on the horizon, the people awoke from their stupor and remembered their families waiting at home. There was homework to be done, dinners to prepare and children to bathe. They had completely forgotten about their day-to-day lives for just a moment. Visiting the Garden of Four Seasons was like going on a wonderful holiday.

Mrs Lu's Teahouse

News of the amazing garden in Rumba Street travelled like an infectious yawn in the span of just a few short days. Even the neighbourhood dogs, downwind of the garden, smelt something delicious in the air and whined at their gates to be let out.

Mrs Lu was surprised at all the people outside her shop. Mimi often drew on the footpath, but never had there been such interest.

Ding ding-a-ling.

'Hello, Mrs Lu,' said Mr Honeybun, his bald head popping into the shop. 'You have a real little Picasso there. This is my third visit in two days and I still haven't seen it all.'

'Seen what all, Mr Honeybun?' asked Mrs Lu.

'Why, the Garden of Four Seasons. You haven't seen it yet?'

Mrs Lu came out of the shop, curious to see what all the fuss was about. She cast her eyes over the garden drawn so beautifully on the grey paving stones. Instantly, memories of her life in China during the 1960s returned.

She saw herself, a young girl in Hangzhou. Her hair in neat plaits, a red scarf tied around her neck. It was the time of the Cultural Revolution. Out in the street, a loudspeaker was spitting out slogans, '*Be good children for Chairman Mao. He is the bright, golden sun. Study hard and you will go to the top.*'

Through the lattice window of her bedroom, she could see a ginkgo tree. Its fan-shaped leaves fell to the ground like golden snowflakes. The ginkgo is one of the oldest species on earth. It has survived three hundred million years, since before the dinosaurs. The young girl loved this ancient tree as much as she loved Chairman Mao, the leader of China. Everyone loved Chairman Mao. Some children loved him even more than they loved their own parents.

Mimi opened a drawer in the medicine cabinet and grabbed a handful of tiny red berries to snack on. When she turned around, there was the smiling face of Josh Rudd on the other side of the counter. He was dressed in baggy khaki pants and an orange shirt. His fair hair was gelled to look intentionally untidy.

'Hi, M.'

'Um . . . What are you doing here?' Mimi stumbled over the words and her face flushed red with embarrassment. Seeing him outside of school felt awkward and unnatural.

'I came to see the garden. It's so cool!'

'Thanks.' Mimi looked down at the berries in her hand. *Come on, say something, otherwise he'll think you're a real idiot.* 'Ah . . . want to try some?' She held out her hand.

'Sure, what are they?'

'*Go Ji Zi*. Good for the eyes.'

'Got anything for untidiness?'

Mimi giggled. 'No herbs are that strong.'

Mrs Lu came scurrying back inside.

'Mum, this is Josh. He goes to my school.'

'Hello, Josh.' She put on her glasses and looked him up and down. 'You nice strong boy, come with me.' Mrs Lu dragged Josh by the arm to the kitchen.

'What are you doing, Mum?' Mimi had never seen her mother as excited as this before.

'I open teahouse just like in Hangzhou. Many thirsty customers outside. Dragon Well Tea is best in China, my dumplings best in Australia. Daddy not come back for one week. Can make a little money this way.'

'People won't like tea and dumplings, Mum. It's so . . . so . . . Chinese. Everyone drinks cappuccinos. You should open a café. I'll make chocolate cake . . .'

'I think a Chinese teahouse is a great idea,' said Josh. 'It'll be a goer for sure, Mrs L.' He gave Mrs Lu a thumbs-up.

Mimi still thought it was a bad idea, but her mum's heart was set on it and Josh, well, he did think it was kind of cool.

From under the stairs, Josh pulled out two folding mahjong tables and eight chairs and set them up in the front of the shop while Mrs Lu began making dumplings. First she made the dough from flour and water, then rolled it into balls. Each ball was then flattened out to form a perfect circle. The filling was made from vegetables chopped up finely and mixed together with a generous lashing of soya sauce, sesame seed oil and a dash of sugar. Mrs Lu's fingers worked fast as she folded the dumplings. They looked like little men sitting with outstretched arms, their fat bellies resting on the table.

She saw Josh watching her intently. 'Come on, you try.'

He followed Mrs Lu step by step but his first attempts looked nothing like dumplings.

'They look like grey lumps of dog vomit,' Mimi whispered in his ear.

Josh threw a handful of flour at her. Mimi ducked and the powdery missile hit Mrs Lu smack on the side of the face.

'Sorry,' Josh said.

Mrs Lu laughed. Then Mimi laughed. 'It no matter, Josh,' she said, wiping her face with her upper arm. 'Flour good for skin,' and she rubbed it in so that her face was as white as a Chinese opera singer's. 'Your dumpling now look like podgy little caterpillar, but one day they change into beautiful butterfly like mine.'

Mrs Lu placed the dumplings into a giant five-tiered bamboo steamer and put it on the gas stove. Soon the kitchen was filled with a delicious smell. Steam belched through the woven lid like a dragon all fired up.

Mimi made a sign which read:

Mrs Lu's Teahouse
Serving
Vegetarian Dumplings
Healthy Herbal Soups
Dragon Well Tea

The Garden of Four Seasons and the Teahouse were an instant success. People viewed the garden, then went in for a refreshing cup of tea. Some neighbours met for the first time, even though they had lived in the same street for decades.

They would say, 'Hello, your face seems familiar. Live around here?'

'Yes . . . Tango Street,' would be the reply.

'We're neighbours then.'

'Well, fancy that. I hear the dumplings are sensational here. Want to join me for a cuppa?'

'Why not.'

Mimi enjoyed being a waitress, especially with Josh's help. He made people laugh with his dazzling style of serving. As he weaved in and out of the tables with a tray of food held high in one hand above his head, he yelled, '*Lai le, Lai le. Food's here.*' He said he saw it in a Chinese movie once.

The *Wattle Valley Whisper* wrote an article all about Mimi.

Rumba Magic

TWELVE-year-old Mimi Lu, a Wattle Valley Primary School student, is a talent to watch. Mimi has drawn a garden so real on the footpath in Rumba Street that people come from all over the city to see it. 'I call it the Garden of Four Seasons,' Mimi said. Shopkeepers in the area say business has never been better. 'They all want to see the garden,' said Vic Taranto, owner of Vic's Greengrocery. 'It's hard to get a parking space so people leave their cars at home and walk. It's the best thing that's happened to this little community.' Mimi's enterprising mother has opened Mrs Lu's Teahouse where she serves Chinese tea and dumplings. It's well worth a visit.

Mr Honeybun sat at one of the tables sipping green tea from a small porcelain teacup.

'Taste sweetness in back of throat, Mr Honeybun.' Mrs Lu set down a plate of steaming dumplings.

He took another sip and his eyebrows shot up like two bushy possum tails.

'Yes, I can indeed,' he said. 'The tea is sweet.'

'My dumplings very good, you try,' said Mrs Lu. She stood back waiting for his reaction.

He picked up his chopsticks and chased a dumpling around the plate as if it were alive.

'You gotta stab it, Henry,' said Alma sitting behind him on the next table. She made short thrusting motions with her hand.

'Thank you, Alma,' he said, politely nodding. He successfully skewered the dumpling. It dribbled with juice. 'Mm . . . delicious, Mrs Lu.'

For the past year, Mr Honeybun had wanted to ask Alma out, but he was shy about his plastic leg. This would be the perfect occasion. Mr Honeybun turned to face her, then quickly turned back again. She was putting on her lipstick. Maybe some other time.

Mimi saw Miss O'Dell come into the shop.

'Did you see it, the garden I mean?' she asked excitedly. 'The pastels are amazing . . .'

'Shhh . . .' Miss O'Dell gently cut her off then whispered, 'Let's make it our secret, Mimi. Remember . . . they can be very dangerous in the wrong hands.'

'Oops. Sorry . . . I forgot.'

'I came to see if you wanted to draw a mural on the art-room wall. What do you think?'

'I'd love to,' Mimi replied. 'When can I start?'

'First thing after assembly tomorrow morning.'

Mimi didn't dawdle to school the next day. She couldn't believe she was allowed to miss maths to work on something she *really* loved.

She opened the box of Empress Cassia Pastels and drew a waterfall tumbling into a crystal-clear waterhole. Three toffee-coloured children sat on the sandy bank, kicking their feet in the shallows and laughing. In amongst the ferns and tall trees of the rainforest, colourful birds and animals watched them playing. The mural seemed to quiver as life stirred within.

'Hi there, Smelly-Loo. Quite a celebrity now, aren't you?' It was Gemma.

Mimi pretended to take no notice.

'You think you can make everyone like you by doing these drawings, but don't forget, underneath it all, you're still the same old Smelly-Loo who lives on top of a smelly old shop.'

Mimi kept on drawing. There was silence, but she could still feel Gemma's presence behind her.

Instead of concentrating on Mimi, Gemma stood looking at the mural now. She stepped back to take in the beautiful world drawn on the wall then came up close to inspect a minute detail. Gemma was intrigued. She looked down at the box of pastels sitting on the purple silk scarf. Suddenly, a shimmer of light passed over them.

Startled, Gemma looked at the pastels, then at the mural, then at the pastels again and then at Mimi. A devious smile pricked the corners of her mouth. 'I get it now. It's *not* you . . . you're not that good . . . it's those . . . those . . . crayon thingamies.'

Mimi stopped drawing and picked up the box protectively.

Bing bing bing bing. The lunch bell rang. As the teachers and children filed out of the classrooms, Gemma turned and walked away.

Everybody stood in front of the art-room wall, looking at the picture in silent wonder. It took every bit of their concentration. Then a Grade One said, 'Shhh! Listen.'

'What?' asked a Grade Five.

'Splashing and giggling. Can't you hear them?'

'Yes, I can,' said a Preppy.

'I can too,' whispered another.

'They're pretending to be seals,' shouted another.

'We can hear the bats screeching,' said the twins together.

Soon all the children could hear. The mural had come to life for them. There was a buzz of excitement, like bees finding the first nectar blooms of spring.

'Children have such *vivid* imaginations,' said Principal Cooper. 'But I must admit . . . the mural does look almost real.'

The other teachers nodded in agreement. All except Miss O'Dell. She, like the children, could hear it too.

The Garden of Empress Cassia

Mimi lay under her silk-filled duvet and gazed out of the window at a pair of tiny bright eyes in the morning sky. The stars winked at her. The purr of the traffic was becoming a roar. It was six o'clock.

On her bedside table lay the Empress Cassia Pastels. *Funny how they look so new. Will they never wear down?* She read the last part of the inscription again; *A Treasure for Some A Curse for Others.* Mimi knew how much of a treasure they were, but why would they be a curse?

The telephone rang in the next room.

'*Wei*,' said Mrs Lu, answering in Chinese. 'Aiya . . . Poor Ting.'

Mimi guessed it was her dad. 'He has no wife, no children, only us.' Mrs Lu sighed again. 'It was good you were there with him at the end. You'll be home on Thursday then? Yes, I understand . . . after the funeral.'

Mimi lay in bed, trying to remember Uncle Ting's face. It was as though she were looking into a pond and raindrops were falling on to the surface, blurring the contours. But Mimi was certain that the two stars winking through the window were the bright eyes of her uncle. She looked out into the blue-black morning sky and whispered, 'I'll miss you not being on Earth, Uncle Ting, even though I haven't seen you for ages. I wish I had a photo of you. I can't remember what you look like any more. If you're reborn like Mum says we all are, I hope you come back and live close by. Maybe you can give me some kind of sign. Goodbye, Uncle Ting.'

Mimi dressed quickly and went outside. *Good, just enough morning light to start.* She knelt on the footpath outside Vic's Greengrocery. Even though her mind was empty she felt as though there was something huge inside her heart – something very special wanting to come out. She opened the lid of the pastels. In an instant, a magnificent garden formed like a dream before her eyes. Mimi took a deep breath, chose a pastel the colour of an autumn day and began to draw the Garden of Empress Cassia.

The twelve o'clock tram clattered down Rumba Street when Mimi drew the final stroke on the footpath. The drawing was complete. She stood up to get a bird's-eye view. The garden was so beautiful that even Mimi herself was taken completely by surprise. Every tiny detail was exact and the colours as brilliant as if the garden were alive. Suddenly, there was a loud shriek from behind her.

'Watch out!' someone hollered.

Mimi collided with a big, bulky body coming in the opposite direction. She fell to the ground, painfully landing on her knees – the wind knocked out of her. It took a few moments to catch her breath – then her eyes focused on a walking stick, a pair of familiar black shoes and two pillar-like legs. It was the dreaded Miss Sternhop.

'Miss Stir-em-up . . . I mean Sternhop . . . I'm sorry.'

Mimi felt the Sternhop glare piercing her head and zapping her brain cells.

'Stupid child, why don't you look where you're going and what's this graffiti on the footpath?' Miss Sternhop's voice sliced the air like broken pieces of glass.

Mimi's heart beat wildly in her chest as she replied, 'It's a g-garden – the Garden of Empress Cassia.'

'And what's this?' Miss Sternhop tapped at some words with her walking stick, then read slowly.

'*Under your feet the journey begins. In the palm of your hand the journey ends. Come, enter the space between Heaven and Earth.* What space? *What* journey? *What rubbish, child!*' She began rubbing away the words with her foot.

'Miss Sternhop, don't!' cried Mimi, suddenly fearful. But it was too late. Miss Sternhop was slowly being sucked into the garden!

'Oh dear, what's happening? *HHHEEELLLLLPPP!*' The frightened voice grew fainter and fainter.

'Hold on, Miss Sternhop, I'm coming,' Mimi yelled, jumping in after her.

Miss Sternhop landed on her back with a soft *flumph*, her feet and arms waving in the air like an overturned turtle. Mimi went to help her up.

'Oh my, what a beautiful place,' Miss Sternhop said in an unusually soft and sweet voice.

'It's the Lake of Secret Dreams,' said Mimi. Even though she knew every detailed stroke of the garden, this was the first time she had been inside one of her own drawings. She looked about her in wonder. It was so real.

All along the shore, willow trees dipped their long green plaits into the lake, while lazy goldfish kissed the underside of the water looking for insects. Miss Sternhop sat down on a rock and gazed across the garden to the mountains in the distance. Her body melted into each hole and crevice. No longer was she the stiff, stern lady Mimi once knew.

'Would you like to explore the garden?' asked Mimi.

'Yes indeed,' replied Miss Sternhop.

The garden was vast, like a kingdom unto itself, with tall mountain peaks, delicate pavilions and bridges criss-crossing the lake. Mimi and Miss Sternhop wandered through the Forest of Gentle Ghosts and explored Laughing Hole Grotto. Then they climbed up a thousand and sixty-five steps to where Crimson Cloud Temple stood carved into the side of a steep mountain cliff. There they rested on the terrace, while shiny-headed monks in grey robes served them tea and sweet date cakes.

The Garden of Empress Cassia was completely surrounded by a long wall, its top snaking like a flying dragon. In the wall, fan-shaped windows framed a mountain view or a creamy-white peony flower. And along the wall's surface were carved all kinds of dragons flying between clouds of the softest pink. Mimi and

Miss Sternhop came down off the mountain, laughing and giggling. But when Miss Sternhop saw the wall, the laughter faded from her face. She stared at the flying dragons and her eyes filled with tears.

'What's the matter, Miss Sternhop?' Mimi couldn't believe she was crying. In class she had tried to imagine Miss Hilda Sternhop as a baby. A fat baby with tight, thin lips. Baby Hilda never cried, just screamed. '*MO . . . THER . . .* I'm awake, change my nappy, where's my milk, give me my dummy, get me up, shake a leg –'

Mimi now knew that *anything* was possible in the Garden of Empress Cassia.

'I was remembering Beechwood,' said Miss Sternhop. 'The time when a two-seater plane made a crash landing in Main Street. I was your age, twelve or thirteen years old. The plane barely missed Mrs Hatchet's old red pick-up truck, just scraping her roof with its wheels. The pilot was very clever though, swerving this way and that to avoid the cars – and finally ending up with the plane's propeller in the dust. As he climbed out of the cockpit, everyone cheered and all the men went up to shake his hand and pat him on the back as if he were a hero. He was very handsome. I raced home to tell my father. Nothing exciting ever happened in Beechwood.

'I told him how brave the pilot was and that I wanted to fly when I grew up. I've always wanted to fly. I would lie in the sunflower field beside our house and watch the wedge-tailed eagles gliding effortlessly in the sky.

'My father scolded me. Called me ridiculous. "Girls don't fly aeroplanes!" he said. "Teaching. Now that's a nice profession for a girl."

'In those days, girls obeyed their parents and had few choices about what they were going to do. That was the last time I talked about flying to anyone . . . until now.'

Mimi put her hand into Miss Sternhop's. She led her across a zig-zag bridge to a pavilion in the middle of the Lake of Secret Dreams. The black-tiled roof looked like an elegant hat worn at the races. Miss Sternhop walked up the steps.

'The Pavilion of the Mysterious Way –' Miss Sternhop read. She wondered for a second how she could read the Chinese characters.

Together Mimi and Miss Sternhop sat on the wooden seat that circled the inside of the pavilion. They both had secret dreams and understood each other perfectly.

Ding, ding, ding. The twelve o'clock tram rattled noisily down the street, leaving behind a swirl of dust. Not a nanosecond had passed in the *outside* world on

Rumba Street since Miss Sternhop was sucked into the garden. She stood on the footpath, relaxed, her weight on one leg. She didn't remember her journey. But as she leant down to pat a small child on the head, Mimi knew that Miss Sternhop had changed inside.

'Goodbye, Mimi,' she said. 'Now where did I put my walking stick?'

'Maybe you won't need it any more,' Mimi said.

'You know, I don't think I will.' Miss Sternhop walked up Rumba Street as if she were on a brand new pair of legs.

The next day was one of those hot, stuffy southern hemisphere days, when the north wind blows so warm it's hard to breathe. Even the flies were too lazy to move and stuck to the skin like leeches.

'Hello, my old China plate,' greeted Mr Honeybun. 'It's going to be a real stinker today.'

'Close your eyes,' said Mimi, 'and I'll take you somewhere nice and cool.'

Mr Honeybun was always in for a bit of fun, so he closed his eyes and put out his hand. Mimi led him to the words written on the pavement where the entrance of the garden stood.

'Stand here and read this, Mr Honeybun. You'll be there in a flash.'

Mr Honeybun read, '*Under your feet the journey begins. In the palm of your hand the journey ends. Come, enter the space between Heaven and Earth.*' As soon as he had finished reading, he vanished into the garden.

The next visitor to happen down the street was a hot and bothered Mrs Jacobs in her red high-heeled shoes. Every few steps she stopped to wipe her brow and brush away the flies.

'Hello, dear, what have you drawn this time?'

'Another garden, Mrs Jacobs.'

'Oh, I do love gardens –' She felt a cool breeze blowing across the footpath.

'Perhaps the change is on its way already. Is this a poem, dear?'

'Yes, Mrs Jacobs.'

Mrs Jacobs read the inscription and, like Miss Sternhop and Mr Honeybun, was whisked into the garden. Mimi followed her in.

Mrs Jacobs breathed in the scent of lilacs, then walked dreamily towards the Pavilion of the Mysterious Way. The breeze blew cool against her face.

She turned and smiled at Mimi. 'George gave me a

blue sapphire ring when I was sixteen. It was too big for my finger, so I wore it around my neck on a strand of wool. The following year, he bought me a gold chain to match.' Mrs Jacobs sighed and touched her neck as if she could still feel it there. 'I lost it years ago . . . the only gift I ever really treasured you know.'

'Kristel —' came a voice from across the lake.

Mrs Jacobs looked around bewildered. 'George? George, is that you?'

'Yes, Kristel. I have something to tell you.'

A watery image of a man drifted over the lake and into the pavilion like a mirage.

George bent down and kissed Kristel on the cheek — then whispered something in her ear. She nodded slowly with a smile.

'I knew it. I just knew it was somewhere safe. Thank you, love.' The ghost-like figure of George drifted back across the lake and gradually vanished into the mist.

As Mrs Jacobs left the Pavilion of the Mysterious Way, Mr Honeybun was coming up the steps. They didn't greet each other, even though they were old friends. It was as if they were in the garden all by themselves.

There were other people there too. All walking around enjoying the beauty, all lost in their own thoughts. Mimi saw Mr Holes sitting in the bamboo grove, reading. She was glad he had come to visit.

Mimi stood on the footpath beside Mrs Jacobs. They had just emerged from the garden.

'Now, what were we talking about? Oh, yes, your new garden. It's a lovely drawing, dear.' Mrs Jacobs didn't remember anything about her visit – but then she put her head to one side and a puzzled expression came over her face.

'Something . . . something I need to remember . . . something to do with George. Now, what was it?'

Suddenly, her face lit up and her eyes sparkled. '*My ring!* I remember now. George and I went on a trip to Tassie in seventy-eight. Before we left, I hid the ring in the cellar behind two loose bricks. Fancy that, remembering after all these years. It must be the hot weather, although I feel as cool as an ocean breeze.' She lifted her head and looked up to the sky. 'Thank you, love . . . I must go home right away. Bye, Mimi dear.'

A few days later, Mimi saw Mr Holes walking past the shop. She hardly recognized him without his holey coat and beard. He wore jeans and a checked shirt and his dreadlocks were half their original length. Now they looked like spaghetti springs. Mimi was surprised by how young he really was – about twenty years old.

'I'm going back to uni,' he said.

'I didn't know . . .'

'Yeah, I'm going to finish my law degree. My parents have taken me back in, so I'll be living at home for a while. They live on the other side of town but I'll come by and say hello from time to time. Later, kiddo.'

'Yeah, see ya, Mr Ho . . . hey, what *is* your real name?'

'It's Ed,' he called back with a wink and a wave.

Awakening the Dragon

Mrs Lu's Teahouse
is closed today for
Chinese New Year.
Happy Year of the Dragon!

Mrs Lu sat on Mimi's bed and handed her a small red New Year envelope. 'Wow, forty dollars! Thanks, Mum . . . it was only twenty last year.'

'I know, but you born in Year of Dragon. I give you double lucky money. Get ready for parade now. It start at eleven.'

'But I don't want to go. Can't I skip it this year? Dad won't know.'

Every year Mimi was forced to march in the

New Year Dragon Parade and she hated every second of it. Imagine if she saw someone from school! She'd just die of embarrassment.

'Dragon bring us good luck,' said Mrs Lu. 'Look, you wear my wedding dress. It fit you for sure.' She held up a simple red silk dress with a high collar and tiny embroidered butterflies dancing across the front.

'There is someone at door. I go, you try on,' she ordered.

Mimi reluctantly put on her mum's dress. *Makes me look really Chinese now*, she thought with disgust, catching sight of her reflection in the mirror.

'Look who's here.' Mrs Lu walked into the bedroom followed by Josh. 'He come to be leg of Dragon.'

'Hiya, M. Hey, you look great! Like a Chinese princess.'

'I don't want to look like a Chinese princess,' Mimi said, annoyed.

'So pretty,' added her mum, pulling Mimi's hair into a high ponytail.

She wriggled away. 'I feel stupid in this. I'm not going.'

'Aiya,' grunted Mrs Lu.

'Come on, M. It'll be cool fun,' said Josh.

'But I'm so sick of it. Everyone stares and points at you. I feel like a real idiot.'

'You're so lucky having something like this. It's a great excuse for a party. My family were poor convicts dragged to Australia in chains. Nothing to celebrate there. Come on, we can have a pizza later. What do you say?'

'All right then . . . at least I won't look stupid all by myself.'

The Dragon lies sleeping in an old warehouse in China-town. He has not stirred for one whole year. The Dragon has the head of a camel, the horns of a deer, the beard of a goat, the scales of a fish, the teeth of a tiger and the tail of a carp. He is strength and power. The Dragon brings rain and good fortune and now he is about to be awakened.

Every year Old Ma was invited to perform the special ceremony. He was one hundred and seven years old. Being a Taoist and practicing the ancient art of feng shui, he knew many secrets about life and one of these secrets was waking up dragons. He stood in front of the altar table filled with wine, tea, meat and fruit – a tiny figure in a business suit, holding a bundle of incense.

'What's all that food for?' whispered Josh, standing next to Mimi dressed in black kung-fu pants and a T-shirt with a dragon design swirling down the front. He fiddled with the red sash around his waist.

'It's for Guan Gong, keeper of the Dragon.'

'Who's he?'

'A kind of god. He was a general who lived in China hundreds of years ago. That's a picture of him there on the table.' It was a painting of a big man with a red face and black beard.

The incense sticks were lit. Smoke curled upwards and the fragrance of sandalwood filled the warehouse. Old Ma bowed three times then began a special prayer in Chinese.

'Today is Chinese New Year. The Dragon is coming out to bless the people and chase away evil spirits. Here is an offering to thank you, Guan Gong, for keeping the Dragon safe all year long while he slept.'

'What's he saying?' whispered Josh.

Mimi shrugged her shoulders and smiled. 'It's all Greek to me. He's speaking in another dialect.'

Old Ma turned to the Dragon. He dipped a paint-brush into fresh pig's blood. The crowd held its breath as the little man stood on the tips of his toes to whisper in the Dragon's ear. Then, with great precision, he first dotted one eye – then the other. The great beast was awakened.

Everyone gave a cheer and the big drum beat out an exciting rhythm as the dancing lion approached. But instead of moving aside to let them through, as was the custom, Old Ma remained looking into the Dragon's eyes, a puzzled expression on his wrinkled face. Then, as though following the Dragon's gaze, he turned around slowly and stared straight at Mimi. She felt as though his eyes were looking inside her brain.

She couldn't move. She couldn't breathe. Everything seemed to be in slow motion, even the beating of the drum.

Suddenly, the lion leapt into the silent space between Old Ma and Mimi, breaking the spell, one man under the head, the other under the tail. The lion's orange tasselled mane danced through the still air like shooting flames.

'Hey, M, we'd better go. They're calling us.' Josh nudged her.

'What? Oh . . . OK,' she replied, as if waking from a dream. She craned her neck to catch another glimpse of Old Ma but the warehouse was crowded with people following the Dragon through the doors on to the street.

Mimi joined the other girls at the head of the parade. She carried a papier mâché horse on a long bamboo pole. Other girls carried colourful flower lanterns made out of silk. Josh marched along at the back with the boys, carrying a ceremonial sword. He was too young to be a leg for the Dragon.

A man, dressed in yellow silk, teased the Dragon with a woven bamboo ball on a long pole. He waved it in front of the Dragon's nose, leading it on. This was the Pearl of Wisdom and no dragon could resist it.

The procession wound its way through the narrow streets of Chinatown. Firecrackers danced around Mimi's feet, exploding into tiny orange sparks. But she didn't notice or hear a thing – she was still thinking about Old Ma.

'You Mimi?' came a muffled voice beside her.

'What?' she asked, taking a wad of cotton wool out of her ear.

A person in a pig mask carrying a rake repeated, 'You Mimi?'

'Yes, I am.'

'Got a message for you then.' The pig handed her a piece of paper then melted into the crowd.

Mimi unfolded the note:

URGENT.
Meet Mr Ma
12 Celestial Lane, Chinatown.
Tomorrow.

How strange. What could he want? Mimi was both fearful and excited at the same time.

The Dragon Parade entered the main street of China-town and stopped under the Facing Heaven Gate. Mimi didn't even notice the two-storey string of firecrackers waiting to be lit for the grand finale. She was looking for Old Ma.

All of a sudden, the silence was broken by the *phut, phut* sound of firecrackers, each cracker setting off another in a chain reaction. Then, as suddenly as it began, the noise stopped. The Dragon parade was over for another year. Next year would be the year of the Snake.

Back at the warehouse, Mimi changed quickly and went to find Josh. She couldn't wait to show him Old Ma's strange note. She found him waiting by the door.

'How much fun was that?' he said. 'I'm coming next year for sure. I'll bring the whole gang from school.'

'Yeah. I enjoyed it too, for the first time ever. Come on, let's go get a pizza. I've got something to tell you.'

As they sat in the restaurant eating pizza, Mimi told Josh about Old Ma and showed him the curious note. What she didn't show him was how scared she felt. She wanted to ask him to go with her, but this was something she knew she had to do alone.

The Story of Empress Cassia

Mimi walked into the shop at number twelve Celestial Lane, Chinatown. Pillars of gritty books and magazines towered on dusty shelves. One tap would have sent them flying.

'Yes?' came a rude voice from behind the counter.

'I'm looking for Old Ma.'

A red-nailed finger whipped out of the darkness and pointed to the steep wooden stairway at the back.

Mimi made her way cautiously through the passage of books. The stairs reminded her of home. Steep and creaky. At the top was a long hall with doors off to both sides.

She called out timidly, 'Mr Ma, are you there?'

'Eh!' came a raspy voice from the room on the left.

Old Ma sat in a leather armchair, horse hair bursting from its seams. His body was so small and the chair so big and clumsy, in the dim light he looked as though he were perched in the mouth of a giant hippopotamus. At that moment he didn't look scary at all. Mimi caught a giggle in her throat and covered a smile with her hand.

'Some cassia tea?' Old Ma spoke in a voice like rusty old nails. He reached over to the small brass table where an earth-coloured teapot and two teacups as thin as eggshells stood. The sweet scent of the cassia flower filled the musty room as the pale yellow liquid slipped like silken honey into the tiny cups. With a knobbly, stiff hand, he nudged one over towards Mimi then looked deep into her eyes.

'Yesterday, I wake Dragon. He open eye and look at someone in crowd. I very surprise. I turn around, see face of girl. I see Garden of Empress Cassia. Is this true, Mimi? You have seen garden . . .?'

'Yes, it's true, Mr Ma. The garden is on the footpath near my house. I drew it with the Empress Cassia Pastels.'

Old Ma sank back into his hippopotamus armchair. 'At last . . .' he sighed. 'I wait so long – so many hundred years.'

Mimi was curious to know if it was just Old Ma's poor English or had he really lived *many hundred years*?

'Have you heard story of Empress Cassia?' he asked, before she had time to ask his age.

'Was she a real empress?'

'She live long time past in China.'

'Was she beautiful?'

Old Ma nodded. 'Most beautiful in land. She have rosebud lips and wide eyes and hair black like night. She live in big palace with much servants and wear yellow gown of Empress. When she eleven year old, her father, big brave Emperor Wu, die in battle against barbarians. Very sad. But Cassia clever girl. She ride horse and shoot arrow straighter than best archer. Swim faster than great sea dragon in Western Cave – and paint like wind dancing on Lake Taihu. She have big heart. Every night, palace gates open wide for great feast. On twelfth birthday people give her present.'

'What was it?' Mimi sat on the edge of her chair.

'Box of beautiful pastels.'

'The Empress Cassia Pastels . . . of course!' exclaimed Mimi. 'Cool. But they couldn't be the same ones I have.'

'Only one box in whole of world.'

'But they . . . they still look like new,' Mimi said in disbelief.

'They magic pastels, from ancient world. Empress Cassia draw on throne room wall,' he continued. 'She draw plan of beautiful garden. On sixteenth birthday, Garden of Empress Cassia built behind palace. It was garden of perfect balance with long Dragon Wall all around. Every day, Empress Cassia gallop to Pavilion of Mysterious Way. She feed and talk to fish that live in Lake of Secret Dreams.

'One day, General Hu, head of army, rush into throne room. "Barbarians attack from north. Break through Great Wall!"

' "How close?" ask Empress Cassia.

' "Two-day ride. Our army not strong enough."

'Empress Cassia slowly sip cassia tea. She do this to think. "Get all people from city and take to garden. We wait for barbarian there," she ordered.

'Two day pass, barbarian arrive at palace wall, smash down gate. But everywhere, empty. Not even crunchy cockroach left crawling on kitchen floor.

' "Burn to ground!" Big Barbarian Chief cry. They burn down palace.'

'Then what happened?' asked Mimi, holding her breath.

'Barbarian enter garden. Big Barbarian Chief raise sword over Empress Cassia.'

'No!' cried Mimi, her hand over her mouth.

'But wait . . . very strange thing happen. No strength in arm. Sword heavy like five elephants. Big Barbarian Chief get sleepier and sleepier. Whole army fall to ground, snoring like bear in winter cave.'

'Coo-el,' Mimi laughed. 'What happened then?'

'When they wake, they forget where they come from. They think they army for Empress Cassia. Big Barbarian Chief become most loyal general. Peace again all over China. Empress Cassia live very long life. Old as ninety-three. Day she die . . . garden vanish from Earth.'

'Wow. But how could it? Where did it go?'

'There is space between Heaven and Earth where garden lie like sleeping dragon. Mimi use pastels, garden come back.'

'But why me, Mr Ma?'

'Because you have pure heart.'

'But sometimes I'm really bad. Ask my dad.'

'You just naughty girl sometime, not listen to Daddy,

you not bad. Pastels are like mirror of heart. They not lie. If person is bad, pastels very dangerous so you must always keep them safe and hidden. In every time, pastels wait for just right person to bring Garden of Empress Cassia back. One person like you, Mimi.'

'Is this true?'

'Yes, it has been like this for thousand of years.'

'Mr Ma.' Mimi stood up, her eyes bright. 'Come with me, I'll take you into the garden right now.'

'No, Mimi . . . I cannot,' Old Ma sighed. 'Garden of Empress Cassia only for those who hurting inside. It is garden for healing.'

Mimi sat back, disappointed.

'No matter. In my lifetime I seen many beautiful gardens, Mimi.' Old Ma raised his cup slowly and took a long, noisy sip of cassia tea.

The light suddenly dimmed as the sun sank behind the tall buildings of the city.

'It's late. Mum will worry. Thank you, Mr Ma. I'll come and visit you again.'

'Goodbye, Mimi. And remember – guard pastels well.'

'I will . . . oh, I almost forgot. I made you a present.' She handed Old Ma a small scroll.

As Mimi left the shop, a soft drizzle began to fall. Old Ma slipped off the red ribbon and unrolled the painting. Mimi had drawn the Garden of Empress Cassia for him. A miniature version – but with every tiny perfect detail.

The buzz of wings came to Old Ma's ears. A peacock-blue dragonfly dipped its nose into the Lake of Secret Dreams, then flew out of the painting and into the dusty room.

'Ah . . . Empress Cassia . . . ' he whispered.

Dr Lu's Return

Dr Lu walked home from the train station, a suitcase in one hand, a lidded cane basket in the other. Inside the basket sat Uncle Ting's most loved possession – his gift to Mimi.

The sight that met Dr Lu's eyes as he walked down Rumba Street was so strange, he thought he might have taken the wrong turn from the station. Never had he seen so many people milling outside his shop before. Was there an accident? He started running, the basket bouncing against his leg. As he reached the crowd, the people stepped back to let him through as though he were a great emperor. Some smiled and congratulated him, others just shook their heads in admiration.

'You're back,' said Mrs Lu. 'You must be tired. Have some cassia tea.'

Dr Lu looked around his clinic in surprise. People sat at mahjong tables, eating and drinking. There were Mr Honeybun and Alma sitting together in the corner engrossed in conversation. There were others that Dr Lu didn't recognize at all. And instead of the smell of herbs, the aroma of dumplings and cassia tea filled his nostrils.

'What has happened since I've been away?' he asked his wife in Chinese.

'It's Mimi's wonderful garden,' replied Mrs Lu, wiping her hands on her apron and taking his suitcase from his hand. 'People come to Rumba Street just to see it. I set up a teahouse to make a bit of money while you were away.'

'Business looks good,' he said.

'Mm . . . not bad. I'll get you something to eat.'

'Where's Mimi?'

'In the kitchen eating breakfast.' Mrs Lu turned towards the kitchen and called, 'Mimi, your daddy's home.'

Oh no. He'll go ape when he finds out I've been drawing.

The chair legs screeched angrily against the wooden floorboards as she pushed back her seat.

'Hello, Mimi,' said Dr Lu, walking into the kitchen.

'Hi, Dad.'

'Mummy say you do much drawing.'

'Only a little. But I got A for my English test and forty-seven out of fifty for maths,' she said quickly.

'Mm . . . well . . . no talk school now.'

That's a surprise.

'I bring present from Uncle Ting.'

'Is he still alive then?' Mimi asked with a tinge of hope.

Dr Lu spoke in Chinese, his voice sounded sad and tired. 'No, Mimi, he died in his sleep. He was a good man.' Tears came to Dr Lu's eyes.

He lifted the cane basket on to the kitchen table. 'He wanted you to have this.'

'What is it, Dad?'

'Open and see.'

Mimi lifted the latch and felt something alive pushing from the inside. Slowly, she gave way to the pressure. A small grey-haired dog poked its head through the opening, grunting and whimpering with excitement at being let out at last. His little tail seemed spring-loaded, it wagged so fast. Two bright brown eyes looked up at her like the two bright stars though her bedroom window.

'Uncle Ting?' she whispered in its ear. 'Is that you?'

She lifted the little dog out and held him close. His tummy was soft and pink and covered in grey spots of different sizes. It looked as though his mum had put him out in a gentle rain, belly up, and the raindrops had never washed off. In fact, this was the way he always liked to sleep – trusting the world. The little dog grunted like a piglet sucking sweet milk as Mimi cradled him in her arms and tickled his belly.

'What's his name, Dad?'

'Uncle Ting call him Peppy.'

At that moment Mimi had an urge to do something she had never done before. She hesitated, then she put Peppy down and walked up to her dad and put her arms around him. It was strange at first. They had never hugged – but when she felt him hug her back, it seemed as natural and easy as snuggling under her silk-filled duvet on a cold, wintry night.

Mimi lay in bed, Peppy by her side as though he had belonged to her all his life. From the room next door came the familiar sound of her parents' voices speaking to one another in Chinese.

'What did you talk about with Ting?' asked Mrs Lu.

'Our childhood, the fun we had. Then how different we were. Ting was such a dreamer. As a boy he would sit on the tiled roof of our house reading poetry all day long. I thought he was useless. At least in the end we had the chance to be brothers once more.' Dr Lu paused. 'I'm not going to make the same mistake with Mimi.'

Mimi could feel a warmth slowly melting the icy spaces between father and daughter. A change – greater than her mum's teahouse, greater than her drawings, perhaps even greater than the garden itself – had come over the smelly little two-storey shop at number eighty-three Rumba Street.

The Broken Promise

Mrs Lu was busy in the kitchen, singing Chinese opera and making juicy, fat dumplings. After Dr Lu's return, the clinic sprang back to normal except for one round table by the window with eight chairs. It was when Mrs Lu found herself making dumplings in her sleep that she knew it was time to slow things down. One night she even dreamt that the dumplings sprouted legs and chased her around the kitchen.

Behind the counter, Mimi helped her dad fill out prescriptions. Dr Lu's first patient was Miss Sternhop. She came especially early this morning – because later on that day, she had the most important appointment of her life.

Dr Lu finished feeling Miss Sternhop's pulse and

inspecting her tongue. He wrote on his pad and handed the prescription to Mimi.

Mimi had first weighed out herbs when she was seven years old under the watchful eye of her mother. Then she had needed to stand on four telephone books to see over the counter.

Mimi pulled out a drawer, grabbed a handful of herbs then placed them on a small brass tray the size of a saucer. This was suspended from a thin rod by three strings. The rod was made of bone and had tiny measurements along its surface. Mimi held a pink string attached to the top of the rod between her thumb and index finger. By moving a weight until the rod was perfectly balanced, Mimi could accurately weigh out the herbs.

'Your health very, very good today, Miss Sternhop,' Dr Lu said. 'Your skin so clear, your eyes so bright. You only need herbs to maintain health.'

Miss Sternhop smiled with her tight, thin lips. She glanced down at her watch. 'Oh dear, ten o'clock already? My flying lesson's at twelve!'

'Flying?' asked Dr Lu, taking off his glasses to see if Miss Sternhop was joking.

'Yes, I've been learning to fly a glider, a Blanik. I've wanted to all my life. No engine . . . just the sound of the wind. It's the most wonderful feeling in the world, Dr Lu.' She lifted her head and closed her eyes. 'In the air, I'm as free as an eagle. Today I am going for my licence.'

Miss Sternhop hurried to the door. 'Goodbye, Dr Lu, goodbye, Mimi, wish me luck,' she called, rushing up the street as though she had wings on the backs of her heels.

Dr Lu turned to Mimi. 'Very strange . . . Miss Stern-hop like young woman again. Herbs not that strong.'

'She's been in the garden, Dad.'

'Garden?'

'You know . . . the Garden of Empress Cassia.' Mimi pointed to the street.

'But it only drawing.'

'That's what it looks like, but there are people walking around inside all the time.'

'Walk inside a drawing? I no can believe.'

'The garden can only be drawn with these special pastels that Miss O'Dell gave me. Only people who need to be healed in some way can enter the garden. It sounds weird, I know, but when they come out, they're different. That's why Miss Sternhop has changed. It's been her dream to fly and now she's doing it. After Mr Honeybun went in, he had the nerve to ask Alma out on a date.'

'Why no people talk about inside of garden?'

'That's just it . . . nobody remembers being inside except me. That's probably because I drew it in the first place.'

Dr Lu shook his head in disbelief.

'It's true, Dad. Old Ma says the garden has been around for thousands of years. It's always out there, in the space between Heaven and Earth, waiting for the right person to use the pastels, then the garden comes to life again. This time it was me.'

Mrs Lu carried a tray of fried dumplings from the kitchen.

'Come, try new recipe. Red-bean paste inside,' she said excitedly.

Mimi grabbed a pair of chopsticks and skewered a dumpling. 'Mmm . . . delicious, Mum,' she said as she bit deep into the dumpling's crunchy skin. The smooth, sweet red-bean paste oozed into her mouth. It tasted good.

'Have you been in Mimi's garden?' Dr Lu asked Mrs Lu.

'I stood at the entrance and read the inscription, but nothing happened.'

'That's because you don't need the garden, Mum.'

Ding ding-a-ling. The shop door opened. Gemma followed her mother into the shop.

'Mrs Johnson, please come in. Sit down,' said Dr Lu.

Oh no, what's she doing here? The dumpling in Mimi's mouth suddenly tasted claggy and dry.

'Thank you, Dr Lu. Gemma tells me she's in the same class at school as your daughter. She thought it would be nice if they got together while I have my consultation.'

'Good idea. Mimi, look after Gemma. Take her up to your room.'

'But, Dad, I'm busy. I need to clean up the clinic.'

Gemma walked confidently up to the counter smiling her big fake smile as though she were Mimi's best friend.

'Hi, Mim.' Then she leant over and whispered, 'Thought we could catch up while Mum's having her witchety brew treatment with your dad, Dr Smelly-Loo.'

'What do you want?' Mimi whispered back.

'Hurry up, Mimi, what wrong with you? Take friend upstairs.' Dr Lu waved her away.

'I go make morning tea for you and Gemma,' said Mrs Lu. 'Quickly, go. Your daddy busy.'

Reluctantly, Mimi led the way to her room. *She's up*

to something. What is it? Gemma wouldn't be seen dead with me.

'Cute dog. What's its name?' asked Gemma, plonking herself on the bed.

She put her hand out, but snatched it back quickly when Peppy growled. *Good on you, Peps,* thought Mimi. He was always so placid. She'd never seen him growl at anyone before. *Dogs can sense when someone's bad. I wonder if there's a special bad kind of smell they have too.*

'Nice room,' Gemma said sarcastically. 'Mum bought me a double bed for my twelfth birthday and a hot-pink duvet.' She smirked. 'Hey, you should ask for one too –' she looked around the room – 'on second thoughts, don't think it would fit. Your bedroom's smaller than my wardrobe.'

'Why did you come, Gemma?'

'I was out shopping with Mum, that's all. Why so suspicious?'

'Because I don't trust you.'

'Mimi,' called Mrs Lu from the bottom of the stairs. 'Come down get morning tea.'

'In a minute, Mum.'

'No, come now.'

'All right.' Mimi moved towards the door. 'Come on, Gemma, come downstairs with me.'

'No. I'm going to wait right here,' she replied coldly. 'I won't touch a thing, I promise.' Gemma crossed her heart and looked at Mimi with innocent blue eyes.

'Mimi!' came her mum's voice again.

'Take your time. I'll just play with your pooch while you're gone. Come, Poopy, good boy.' Peppy growled, then jumped off the bed to follow Mimi downstairs.

As soon as Gemma was alone, she began searching the room. *Those pastels will make me famous*, she thought. She looked in the bookshelf, under the bed, in the wardrobe. *I'll be on the front cover of* Gorgeous Girl. *Everyone'll be so jealous. Now, where would she put them?*

Gemma opened the top drawer in the bedside table.

'Yesss!' she cried excitedly, then put her hand over her mouth, wondering if someone had overheard her cry of joy. *It'll be the start of my acting career. Or maybe I'll be a model.*

As Gemma lifted the lid, her mind filled with strange images.

'Wow. Cool.' Gemma closed the box quickly, then stuffed the pastels up her shirt.

She crept downstairs and walked through the clinic. 'I'm going home first, Mum. I just remembered I've got homework to do.' Her mum didn't look up, just waved as Gemma went past.

Mimi came rushing out of the kitchen at the sound of Peppy's frantic barking. He never barked in the clinic. Something was terribly wrong. She put down the tray of drinks and raced up to her room. *Please no, not the pastels*, she prayed. But when she saw the silk scarf lying on the floor where Gemma had thrown it, she felt as though her soul had been stolen as well.

Maybe it's not too late, she thought frantically.

Mimi flew down the stairs two at a time, then out the door and down the street towards Gemma's place. Peppy ran along beside her. All the way she practised her tough-sounding voice – *GIVE THEM BACK, GEMMA. I KNOW YOU TOOK THEM. I WANT THEM NOW.*

She came to a house with a neat path bordered with white roses. Taking a deep breath, Mimi pressed the security buzzer on the wall. She waited.

'Who is it?' came Gemma's voice.

'You know perfectly well who it is, Gemma, *give the pastels back!*'

'Is that you, Mimi? Sorry I couldn't hang around for morning tea, but I remembered I had some homework to finish,' Gemma said innocently.

'Give them back or I'll tell.'

'Look, Mimi, I have no idea what you're on about.'

In desperation, Mimi changed her tone. 'Please, Gemma, Miss O'Dell says they're really dangerous, so did Old Ma. Don't you see? You can't use them. You mustn't use them!'

'I don't know what you're talking about. Have to go now. Seeya.' The speaker went dead.

As Mimi walked home, she felt as though all her bones had splintered and her muscles had turned to jelly. How was she going to tell Miss O'Dell? Old Ma was wrong. She didn't deserve the pastels. She couldn't even look after them properly.

Mimi looked up at the sky, swollen with sombre grey clouds. A flash of lightning. The crack of thunder. Wind lashed the electric power lines, playing them like a guitar. Then, as though the whole force of nature were punishing her, the rain came. Each drop like a silver bullet biting into her skin.

The Curse

Helplessly, Mimi watched through the shop window as the garden slowly dissolved.

The Lake of Secret Dreams, the Pavilion of the Mysterious Way, the Dragon Wall, all became rivulets of murky colour that slipped over the curb and into the storm-water drains that criss-crossed beneath the city. The pastels were lost and now the garden was too. And the rain did not let up until Mimi had cried herself dry.

Josh waved at her through the window, then entered the shop. 'Hiya, M, I'm starved. Is your mum serving dumplings today?'

Mimi turned to face him.

'Hey, what's wrong?' he asked.

'Something terrible's happened.'

'What is it, M?'

Mimi took a deep breath, then, like a dam wall bursting, she told Josh about Miss O'Dell's gift, the curse of the pastels, her meeting with Old Ma, the story of Empress Cassia and the healing power of the garden.

Josh stood listening in disbelief.

'Wow! That's amazing,' he said when she had finished.

'But now,' said Mimi, 'Gemma has stolen the pastels.'

'What? How did it happen?'

'She came to see me and, stupidly, I left her alone in my bedroom.'

'It'll be OK, M. Don't worry. She'll get the guilts and give them back.'

'No, not Gemma. I'm really scared for her. Miss O'Dell and Old Ma said the pastels can be dangerous.' Mimi buried her head in her hands.

'Did they tell you anything about the curse?' asked Josh.

'No. I never asked. What am I going to do?'

Josh stood up. 'I'll go over to Gemma's right now and get them back,' he said with determination.

'It's no use. I tried that already.' Mimi's voice was tired and lifeless.

'What about Miss O'Dell. Have you told her yet?'

'I can't.' Mimi was almost in tears again. 'She trusted me and I broke my promise.'

'But it wasn't your fault. Come on, M, you have to tell her sooner or later.'

'I know,' said Mimi. 'That's what I'm afraid of.' She took a deep breath and sighed then looked at Josh.

'What?'

'I'm scared for Gemma.'

'Yeah, me too.'

'But I also have this bad thought in my head that says *I'm glad, I'm glad, serves her right.* It's horrible . . . You see? I don't deserve the pastels.'

'That just means you're normal,' said Josh. 'If you weren't meant to have the pastels, you wouldn't be able to create the Garden of Empress Cassia, would you? Come on, M, Miss O'Dell has Saturday art class. Let's see her before she goes home.'

Miss O'Dell was busy at the trough, washing palettes and paint brushes. 'Hello, Mimi, hello, Josh. What a pleasant surprise.'

Mimi kept her eyes glued on some paint splashed on the lino floor. 'I have something to tell you.'

Miss O'Dell wiped her hands on a towel and came over to the big wooden table. 'What is it, Mimi?' she asked with concern.

'Gemma's stolen the pastels, Miss O'Dell. I left her alone in my room. I knew I shouldn't have. Now she won't give them back.'

Mimi looked up at Miss O'Dell's face. It still held the same soft, kind expression.

'And the garden . . . it's gone too. The rains washed it away . . . I'm sorry.'

'It wasn't M's fault,' Josh said loyally. 'It was Gemma. She was jealous.'

Mimi's eyes widened. 'Jealous? Why would she be jealous? She has everything.'

'All that attention you got with the garden, that made her plenty jealous, especially when your photo appeared in the paper. And who's the popular one now at school? It's not Gemma.'

'Josh is right, Mimi. It wasn't your fault,' said Miss O'Dell. 'Did you tell her how dangerous they can be?'

'Yes, but it only made her want them even more. You

know Gemma.' Mimi sat down. 'What would happen if she used them?'

Miss O'Dell's face went deathly pale and a shiver ran through her whole body. Mimi and Josh looked at each other in surprise.

It was then that a cold fear for Gemma's safety crept slowly over Mimi as she realized that Miss O'Dell must have used the pastels too. But what was so terrifying that she could hardly speak about it?

A part of Mimi didn't want to know. To her, the pastels were pure and good and beautiful. *How could they be a curse?*

'I used them once.' Miss O'Dell looked out of the window.

'What happened?' Josh asked. 'Was it really bad?'

'Far worse than I could ever have imagined, I'm afraid.'

Mimi and Josh waited for Miss O'Dell to continue.

She turned to face them. 'As a child, I used to spend a lot of time at my grandfather's small cottage in the country. He was a cook on a merchant ship and collected souvenirs from all over the world, which he kept in a tall wooden cabinet at the end of the hall. There were masks made of shells and feathers and mud.

There were strange-shaped bottles, jade cups and statues, bones and necklaces. It was like a museum in a shoebox. The cabinet was always locked. No one was allowed to open it. Only Grandfather had the key. Every time I visited, he would unlock the cupboard, pull out one of his treasures and tell me a story about it. I would never tire of these stories, no matter how many times I had heard them before.

'On a trip to China, he brought back with him a beautiful box of pastels. An old street vendor in Shanghai sold them to him. Grandfather told me that the box sat amongst the dusty old painting brushes, ink-stones and scrolls like a sunflower in a winter graveyard. When he was leaving with the box of pastels under his arm, the old man said, "The pastels are not of this world. They can be a treasure to some, but a curse to others." I don't know if he believed the old man, but Grandfather never lifted the lid, even though I pestered him to do so constantly.

'One day, I found myself alone in the house. Grandfather had left his keys lying on the hall table. I opened the cabinet, took the box down, then lifted the lid. In an instant, my mind filled with nightmarish visions, and even though they were so terrifying, I had to draw them. I couldn't help myself. I went outside to the woods at the back of the cottage where there was a flat bed of rock and began to draw something sinister and horrible. All the while I could feel it laughing at me. I was scared. So scared I ran to the house to hide. But when I thought of Grandfather and how angry he would be when he found out, I put the pastels back in the cabinet and returned the key. The next day, with fear in my heart, I went back to that flat bed of rock. All the plants and bushes within a metre around it had died. And do you know what? Nothing has ever grown there since. It was as though every bit of life had been sucked out of the earth.'

'That's horrible,' said Josh.

'But you're not bad, Miss O'Dell. Why did you draw a garden like that?' asked Mimi.

'I took the pastels when they weren't mine to use. Just like Gemma has. They didn't belong to me. I can see that now. They didn't even belong to my grandfather. When he died, he left me all his treasures. I kept those pastels hidden away for twenty-two years . . . until I met you, Mimi. I knew from that very first day you walked into my class that they belonged to you.'

'And now I've gone and lost them.'

'It might not be too late,' said Miss O'Dell. 'Come with me to the staff room while I ring around.'

There was no reply at Gemma's house. Miss O'Dell then tried Phoebe. Her father answered the phone.

'Phoebe's dad said she went off with Gemma at about four, but he has no idea where to,' said Miss O'Dell as she hung up. 'Mimi, can you think of any place they might be?' She sounded desperate.

Mimi thought for a while, then replied, 'Only the shopping mall. She often hangs out there.'

Josh nodded in agreement. 'If it's attention she wants, then using the pastels in the mall would be the perfect place.'

'Right then. You two try the mall. I'll go over to Gemma's.'

When Mimi and Josh arrived at the mall, it was closing time. The usual stream of shoppers was dwindling to a trickle. The mall was only a small arcade with a row of shops on the inside and another row on the street, but many of the kids from school used it as a meeting place and the empty car park as a skateboard park.

'I'll meet you back here in ten minutes,' said Mimi. 'Hurry!'

'Right,' said Josh.

Mimi searched inside all the shops that were still open then checked the toilets. Gemma and Phoebe were nowhere to be seen. Ten minutes later, she met up with Josh who was shaking his head.

Mimi looked at him in despair. It was getting dark.

'There's nothing more we can do, M,' said Josh. 'We'd better go home.'

'Yeah, I suppose you're right.' Mimi followed like a robot. She was too tired to think any more.

At the top of Rumba Street, they said goodbye.

'Don't worry, M. It'll all work out OK.' Josh tried to sound positive.

As Mimi walked home, she thought how strange it was that everything could be so very good one minute, then turn so very bad the next. *Now I understand what Uncle Ting was talking about. The cycle of change – yin and yang. I wonder how long I have to wait for the cycle to come good again.* She sighed and opened the door of the shop. Peppy danced around her feet, almost doing backflips, his little tail wagging furiously. 'I love you too, Peps.' She picked him up and sat on the stairs. Peppy laid his head on her shoulder. He could feel her sadness.

Mimi sat thinking – *If I was Gemma, where would I go to use the pastels? I would want a place that was quiet, because I wouldn't want to be caught. But then again, I'm such a show-off that I'd want everyone to see my fantastic creation.* Mimi went through a dozen places in her mind. Suddenly, her eyes lit up. *Ghost Gum Park would be the perfect place! Empty on weekdays and packed on the weekends.* 'That's where she is, Peps, for sure.'

She grabbed the torch and told Peppy to *stay*. Only ghosts and crazy people went to Ghost Gum Park at night. A creeping fear began pricking her spine like a million icy needles. Mimi was neither a ghost nor a crazy, but she knew she had to go. She had to save Gemma and, most of all, she had to get the pastels back.

Ghost Gum Park

There was only a fraction of a moon that night, partly covered with streaks of grey clouds with the occasional star struggling to shine through them. Mimi trembled and her teeth chattered as she entered the park. She knew it wasn't from the cold.

As she headed down the main path she saw the huge ghost gum on the rise. Its stark white trunk and branches with long spindly fingers looked like giant arms stretching out to grab any passer-by. Locals called it the hanging tree.

At the south end of the park, the usual trickle of Black Grass Creek had become a raging river. Mimi skidded down through the bushes to a muddy path that ran beside the creek.

The canopy of trees above created an eerie light. Some people said they had seen ghosts of the hanged in the woods down there. *But I don't believe in ghosts*, Mimi reminded herself. She set her mind on her goal – finding Gemma and the pastels.

The smell of onion weed was strong in the air and the rushing water of the creek seemed to be calling her name, *Meeemeeee . . . Meeeeeemeeeeeee . . .*

Then she saw it, the glow of a fire on the other side of the torrent. Two dark figures moving, their long shadows dancing upon the face of the cliff.

Mimi could see why Gemma had chosen this spot. The huge rock face was like a giant TV screen. Any drawing on it could be seen from almost everywhere in the park.

She headed for the bridge which was about half a mile upstream. A sudden high-pitched shout rose above the sound of the rushing torrent.

'Gemma!' Mimi yelled frantically, but her voice was carried away by the wind. She knew there was no time to get to the bridge.

Where Mimi was standing, the creek widened, then cascaded over rocks in a series of rapids. Boulders, like giant bowling balls, had fallen many thousands of years ago from the cliff above. Normally, this was the perfect place to cross, but today the boulders were surrounded by a flood of raging white water. Still, Mimi knew she had to take the chance.

She walked back ten paces, then ran as fast as she could towards the water's edge. Landing on all fours in the middle of the first boulder, she clung on to its slippery surface as white water gushed around her, splashing up and soaking her clothes. *Only two to go*, she told herself. But the next jump was going to be far more difficult. With no run-up, she would have to do a cat leap.

She calmed her breathing down, then pushed off. But her jump was not long enough. She landed hard on the side of the boulder and slipped down its rough surface into the water. A searing pain ripped through her knee. With all her strength, she clawed and clambered back up, then sat on top of the rock nursing her bleeding wound. The pain turned into a throbbing ache. She felt faint.

It's impossible, Mimi thought, as she looked at the last boulder that now seemed so far away. *I'll never make it*. Then she groaned when she realized it was just as far to go back. She felt as helpless as an injured cat on a peak-hour freeway.

Over the roar of the water came another high-pitched shout. Suddenly, she remembered why she was there – the pastels, the garden and Gemma. *Come on, Mimi, you wimp. Get up! You might already be too late.*

Mimi stood up, the white water surging around the foot of the rock. She focused her mind on a spot in the middle of the next boulder, forgetting about the space in between. She counted to three, asked Uncle Ting for help, then took a huge leap. Her feet landed perfectly this time. Gaining her balance, Mimi jumped easily on to the bank.

There was no path this side of the creek – just a ledge sticking out from the cliff. She sidled along, her back flat against the rock until she reached a clearing. She could hear Gemma's voice.

'These pastels are unreal! My garden is just as good as Mimi's.' Gemma stood back, admiring the huge drawing she had created on the rock face.

'I didn't think you could draw as well as that, Gem. Let me have a go,' came Phoebe's impatient voice.

'Stop!' yelled Mimi.

'Hey, Smells, you're just in time to see me put the last stroke on my masterpiece. Tomorrow, when everyone comes to the park, I'll be famous!'

The light from the fire flickered on to the cliff face. An icy finger ran across Mimi's neck and down her spine. Gemma had drawn a dark and terrifying garden. It was like death itself.

'Get away!' Mimi yelled frantically. 'It will suck you in!'

'*What did you say?*' The two girls doubled over with laughter.

'I know it's good, but come on now,' Gemma scoffed. 'You're just jealous because my garden's better than yours.' Gemma held the box of Empress Cassia Pastels high in the air as if it were a trophy. 'I can draw just as well as you can, now these are mine.'

'Hey, Gem, what do the words say?' asked Phoebe, turning her head sideways to decipher the scribbly writing on the rock.

'It's brilliant. Came to me in a flash. Listen.' Gemma touched each word as she read the inscription, '*In the Garden of Darkness all nightmares begin . . .*'

Suddenly, a great mass of clouds rose out of the garden. It had the force and the sound of a gigantic whirlwind. And out of these clouds appeared repulsive serpents with whipping tongues and blood-red eyes. They slithered and twisted and devoured each other.

'*Get away from it, Gemma!*' cried Mimi. But the garden had already begun sucking Gemma into its putrid black mouth that opened and closed like a weeping sore.

Mimi grabbed Gemma by the waist and pulled. It was too late. Gemma's head and arms were already trapped inside the Garden of Darkness.

Under the storming clouds, there was not a blink of wind, only a deathly quiet. Gemma opened her mouth to scream. A long, hoarse groan was the only sound that came out. She looked around in horror at the twisted trees and the bleak landscape. A full moon was rising above a cold, black lake, but there was barely a glow. It was as though a giant web had been spun across the sky.

Gemma tried to run, but the bottom half of her body was still outside the garden. She could feel a pulling and a tugging – on the outside from Mimi and Phoebe, and on the inside from a much more powerful force.

Then she saw something moving in the shadows. A hideous snake-like creature with slimy skin and evil green eyes came crawling and slithering towards her along an undulating wall. She tried to scream. But it was as though her lungs and throat were stuffed with cotton wool. Gemma was helpless.

As it came closer, she could smell its hot and fetid breath on her face like a rotting, flyblown corpse. Then its claws gripped her shoulders, pulling and dragging her down into its jaws.

'Quick, Phoebe, help! I'm losing my grip!' yelled Mimi.

Phoebe fell to the ground and desperately hugged Gemma around the knees.

'It's too strong. I can't hold her either!' Phoebe yelled, as the Garden of Darkness sucked Gemma further and further into its centre.

Mimi suddenly felt a cold hand on her shoulder. She screamed.

'It's only me,' shouted Josh over the tremendous noise.

'Oh, Josh! Just in time. Quick, grab Gemma. The garden's sucking her in.'

Josh held Gemma around the waist, Mimi took her thighs and Phoebe pulled at the ankles. It was a deadly serious tug of war.

'We can't let it beat us — try harder!' screamed Mimi, suddenly feeling herself being pulled towards the garden. 'On the count of three. Let's do it. One . . . two . . . three . . . *PULL!*'

With the very last burst of strength left in them, they finally dragged Gemma free, falling backwards on the ground in an exhausted heap of bodies, arms and legs. They lay there stunned and exhausted.

'What did you see in there?' Phoebe whispered.

But Gemma didn't answer. Her face was deathly pale. Mesmerized with fear, her eyes were still fixed in terror on the writhing mass that was the Garden of Darkness – the beginning of all nightmares.

Mimi felt a drop of rain on her face. Then she felt another and another. She looked up into the darkening sky. The rain fell over the park, splashing the rock face with arrows of water, destroying the garden and cleansing the surrounding earth.

'Let's get outta here. This place gives me the creeps.' Josh pulled his shirt collar up around his neck.

'How did you find us?' asked Mimi, gathering up the pastels.

Josh bent down to help her. 'Eliza knew where Gemma was all the time, but didn't dare tell anyone. Finally, she confessed.'

They walked in silence along the bottom of the cliff towards the bridge that crossed the creek, further upstream. They didn't notice the rain. Gemma was like a zombie. She hadn't uttered a word since being inside the garden.

The creek was still swollen and flowing fast. Josh crossed the bridge first, then Phoebe, while Gemma and Mimi walked side by side after them.

Mimi held the box of Empress Cassia Pastels close to her body. She could feel them, warm and vibrant against her heart. She knew they belonged with her. 'I'll never let you out of my sight,' she whispered. 'My precious pastels. You're a part of me and I am a part of you.' She clutched them even tighter.

She didn't see Gemma's eyes widening into a mad stare, or her sideways glance, nor her hands reaching out. It only took a split second. And by the time Mimi realized what was happening, it was too late. With the anger and fury of a violent tornado, Gemma wrenched the box out of Mimi's hands, ran to the side of the bridge and hurled it into the water. 'Good riddance!' she screamed, as if she could push the pastels under with her voice. 'You vile and evil things. Go back to where you came from.'

Mimi watched in horror as the Empress Cassia Pastels bobbed on the surface for a minute, then were gone, swallowed up by the torrent of raging water.

'Gemma, what have you done?' Mimi cried.

'I've done everyone a favour,' she screamed back.

'But you can't destroy the pastels. Don't you know that? They've been around for thousands of years.' Mimi choked on her tears. She raced back along the creek, searching the water frantically with her eyes, hoping the box would surface again or get caught between rocks. But it was no use. The pastels were lost to her forever.

Mimi walked back to join the others. Tears streamed down her face. She couldn't even hate Gemma. There were no feelings left inside her any more. 'I did you a favour, Mimi.' Gemma's voice was quivering and her body shaking uncontrollably. 'If you'd seen what I saw in that repulsive garden, you'd have done exactly the same thing. I'll have nightmares for the rest of my life.'

Sweet Dreaming

From her bed, Mimi could see the cold, empty space where the Empress Cassia Pastels used to lie. Thoughts tumbled over and over in her mind like waves crashing on the shore. She tossed and turned on her pillow. *They're probably floating in the sea by now,* she thought. *Who'll find them next? I hope it's someone good.* Mimi's only comfort was little Peppy, snuggled into the duvet beside her, belly up, snoring loudly. *And the garden. I won't ever see it again, either.*

The sweet scent of the cassia flower came into the room and a hush silenced her thoughts. Mimi heard the swish of silk, but didn't lift her head from the pillow. A new idea was forming. A shiny, clear thread of a thought: *The garden . . . it is still here . . . it might have gone* back to the space between Heaven and Earth, but it's growing inside all those people. Miss Sternhop, Mr Honeybun, Mrs Jacobs, Mr Hol . . . I mean Ed, and all the others it healed. And if it's in them, it must be in me as well. This thought comforted her.

Peppy twitched and whimpered. 'It's all right, Peps.' Mimi gently stroked him.

So many people have changed because of the pastels and the garden. Gemma won't be giving me a hard time any more, I'm sure of that. Nightmares for the rest of her life — that's punishment enough.

It took Uncle Ting's death to make Dad change. That's pretty drastic. I guess instead of the garden it's Uncle Ting inside him now. Hi, Uncle Ting. You'd be glad to know Dad's lightened up a lot lately. No more pressure about school work. I couldn't believe it when he said he'd take me to a movie . . . That's a first. He's happy now too because I speak Chinese with him. Never realized before but it comes in handy when you don't want other people to know what you're talking about. And Mum's happy, because we both are. That's Mum . . . keeper of the peace.

And Josh? Well . . . he's just cute and nice and sweet and a really, really, really good friend. Best friend I've ever had. Only friend I've ever had except for Miss O'Dell and Peppy.

Mimi's mind was like a covering of freshly fallen snow – all grey thoughts had disappeared. She relaxed into her bed, ready for sleep to come. Then, as a petal of a cassia flower brushed her face, a young girl, with rosebud lips and wearing a gown of the finest yellow silk, walked into Mimi's sweet dreaming.

'Empress Cassia –' she whispered.

'It is here, it is there, all at the one time, Mimi.' The voice was like a bellbird in a quiet mountain forest. 'Can you not see it?' She gracefully flicked back her long sleeve, embroidered with birds and blossoms, then waved her arm as if she were standing in the middle of the garden itself.

Mimi pushed back her duvet and sat up in bed. She looked to where Empress Cassia was pointing, but saw only the blank wall of her bedroom.

Empress Cassia bent down and put her face close to Mimi's. The scent of the sweet flower grew stronger. 'Reach down, deep inside yourself,' she said. 'Let it come . . . come slowly to the surface. The garden is there, but you must help it to grow. When you hear your heart sing – the garden will appear.'

Mimi closed her eyes.

'I can . . . I can feel it,' Mimi whispered, as the garden

welled up inside her. The Dragon Wall, the Lake of Secret Dreams, the mountains and temples and finally the Pavilion of the Mysterious Way played like a movie on the blank wall of Mimi's bedroom.

'Now come. Draw the garden with your heart. You no longer need the pastels.' Empress Cassia took Mimi's hand and together they went out on to the deserted street. It was dark except for the greenish glow of the streetlight. The rain had washed everything clean, leaving a clear, warm summer night.

Mimi could feel every detail of the garden inside her now. And even though the old pastels she used were broken and dull, the lines and colours were just as vibrant as before. The Garden of Empress Cassia was coming to life once more.

'Draw upon it as you will, it never runs dry –' said Empress Cassia. And in that whisper she was gone . . .

The Valley Spirit never dies,
It is called the Mysterious Female,
And the Doorway of the Mysterious Female,
Is the root of Heaven and Earth.
It is there within us all the while;
Draw upon it as you will, it never runs dry.

Lao Tzu 400 BC

About the Author

Gabrielle Wang was born in Melbourne and is third generation Chinese Australian. Her great-grandfather came to Victoria during the Gold Rush in the 1850s. Gabrielle went to art school, then worked as a graphic designer and illustrator, before going to China to study painting. She now writes and illustrates, and teaches Chinese language at RMIT University.

Gabrielle lives in Melbourne with her husband, two children, two guinea pigs, two cockatiels and a small yellow dog, who have all contributed ideas to her stories.